BOOKS BY TIM MCBAIN & L.T. VARGUS
The Violet Darger series
The Victor Loshak series
The Charlotte Winters series
Casting Shadows Everywhere
The Scattered and the Dead series
The Awake in the Dark series
The Clowns

THE
LAST
VICTIM

THE LAST VICTIM

a Violet Darger novella

LT VARGUS & TIM MCBAIN

THE
LAST
VICTIM

CHAPTER 1

November 1993

Her headache throbs. A slow, even pulse of pain.

And a *whoomp* pounds along with it, a choppy sound from within like a helicopter encased in her skull.

Claire feels it. The blood slamming through the veins in her temples, and the muscles there knotting and spasming. It makes her jaw clench and unclench.

Something isn't right. She knows this, but she doesn't know why, doesn't quite know what's happening here.

Wherever she is, she is sleeping. Or was. Can't quite bring herself to open her eyes even now that alarm bells are blaring in her head.

Every thought is a little fuzzy. A little distant.

She tries to focus. Tries to remember or otherwise determine where she is.

The first sensory details occur to her.

Hot and cold.

Warmth radiates in the core of her body. A roiling, angry heat like a broken radiator stuck on full blast.

But a chill touches the flesh of her face. Not a wintry chill so much as that heavy cold that settles over everything in the deep of the night.

Moving.

She is moving. Feels the tug of gravity shift, the

twitch and vibration of motion.

And then the sound fades in.

The white noise of a car engine. Steady. Constant. Yes.

She is in a car.

The realization wrenches something free in her memory. A shard of the night restored all at once.

They'd gone to the bar. Her and Tammy. It was $1 PBR night at The Mystic and neither of them had class in the morning.

She remembered Tammy handing her that third beer, the cold yeasty taste of it on her lips, but after that?

Everything in her head seems to jumble up. A stream of nonsense images. Mundane flashes of people crowding the bar, drinking and talking. Clouds of smoke expanding around goateed faces and then vanishing.

With a little extra prodding, her eyelids peel open at last, one then the other.

She blinks a few times, and the dark blur sharpens around her, revealing her vantage point.

She slumps in the backseat, half lying on Tammy.

Her friend appears to be submerged in a deep slumber of her own, her mouth shiny in the moonlight, slicked with the drool spilling down her chin and pooling on the pewter upholstery.

The silhouette of a man occupies the driver's seat, two hands on the wheel, fingertips drumming lightly. At first she thinks it's Tammy's friend, Eric — the square chin and jaw seem right in profile, but it's too dark. She's not certain.

The idea that this is a stranger lets that chill in her face snake tendrils of cold down into her chest.

Jesus.

She would never take a ride home from a stranger. Never ever.

But Tammy would. Tammy was always getting them into trouble.

And she can't panic. Won't panic. Takes a breath.

She looks out the windows, scans for clues about their location.

The spiky plumage of cholla, yucca, and other cacti populates the side of the road with rocky hills in the background. She can see the looming silhouette of the mountains off to the left. They're on one of the canyon roads, but she has no idea which one it is.

One thing is clear, though: They're moving away from the city.

Away from home.

The blacktop shimmers before them, practically glowing under the glare of the headlights. The yellow lines of reflective paint shining so bright.

None of this makes any sense. At all.

The car slows as it rolls up to a stoplight, and street lamps glint yellow light over them, lighting up the backseat and casting new shadows everywhere.

She blinks a few times, letting her gaze fall to the floor.

An empty pair of Converse All-Stars rests off to the left of where she and Tammy sit. Chuck Taylors. Pink and tiny.

Weird.

Tammy must have taken off her shoes when they climbed into the car. Gotten comfy. She never realized her friend's feet were so minuscule.

Her gaze shifts, however, and she sees the red kitten heels adorning Tammy's limbs.

Yes, of course.

Tammy may own a pair or two of Converse — Claire was pretty sure she did — but she wouldn't have worn them out to the bar tonight. Not her style.

Claire looks at her own feet, wiggling the toes of the Adidas Sambas a little as though to verify that they are her own.

If the shoes aren't Tammy's, and they aren't hers...

Her torso squirms involuntarily, some shuddering of muscles that seems to roll over her in waves. It was almost like her body had made some leap in logic and was waiting for her brain to catch up.

The killer.

The stories on the news about the girls being abducted. Kept for two days. Killed. Burned. The same guy who'd murdered all those girls in Colorado according to the experts.

They didn't even know what he did to the girls. Not exactly. The bodies were all burned too badly to offer forensic evidence.

And one part of her thinks with total certainty that she is crazy. Paranoid. Delusional. Childish.

This isn't a serial killer. It's just some guy that Tammy asked to give them a ride home. Probably someone she knows from one of her classes or something.

But now she is awake.

She watches the dark figure in the front seat as she wriggles into a semi-upright position, peeling her top half away from her unconscious friend.

Apart from those fingers still drumming on the steering wheel, he doesn't move. The glint of the red light shimmering against his pale flesh blinks away to black and then the light comes back green.

The car lurches to life, the engine purring once more.

She gives Tammy a little poke in the ribs with her elbow, prodding lightly at first and then harder the second time.

She hopes her friend will come around slowly, without panicking. They need to get organized without him realizing they are awake.

But Tammy is motionless. Zonked. Totally oblivious to the sharp bone now applying enough pressure to bruise the flesh swaddling her ribcage.

Fuck.

Jesus.

Again that cynical part of her laughs at her fear. Finds it hilarious and egotistical to assume a killer would pick her and Tammy out of the crowd. That anything so dramatic would ever happen to her. Ridiculous.

She moves to grab Tammy's upper arm and give her a shake, but her hands are clumsy. Awkward. She tries again, but they won't quite obey. Almost like they are stuck together.

She stops. Looks.

It takes her a full second to realize that a zip tie fastens her arms at the wrist. Thick plastic. Opaque.

And then she sees Tammy's hands folded as though in prayer, the ring of plastic lashing them together.

She bites her lip to stifle the rush of breath entering her lungs, fights to quiet that telltale gasp.

Because it's not her imagination.

He is going to kill her.

He is going to kill both of them.

CHAPTER 2

Present Day

The most notorious serial killers have a way of shedding their nicknames. At some point, they no longer require them.

Just saying the name "Dahmer" triggers an intense reaction in people. Grisly images, queasy feelings, and all of the graphic details rush into their heads.

The severed head in the fridge.

The heart in the freezer.

Bodies dissolved in acid in a plastic tub in the living room.

The stench permeating the halls, a smell other residents in the building compared to that of chitlins.

By the time these horrors etch their stain onto the public consciousness, a silly nickname like "The Milwaukee Cannibal" has lost all of its power. It seems kitschy and small compared to the real thing.

And like Dahmer, those who reach the highest plane of murderous celebrity become such recognizable brands that their first names can go unmentioned.

Manson.

Bundy.

Gacy.

Dahmer.

Stump.

It was the last of these that Victor Loshak thought about as he waited at a stoplight.

((

Despite the fact that Loshak had specifically requested a non-smoking car, the interior of the rental reeked of stale cigarette smoke. There'd been an air freshener shaped like a pine tree dangling from the rearview mirror when he first got in, but he pitched it before he even started the car. Whatever artificial lemon crap they soaked those things in was probably more carcinogenic than the secondhand smoke baked into the upholstery.

Even with the windows up and the air-conditioner cranked, Loshak could feel the oppressive Nevada heat beating down on the car. There was something about the sunlight in the desert that was different than anywhere else. It was whiter. Hotter. Almost menacing somehow. Perhaps it was some leftover animal instinct that made him want to recoil from the brightness, to seek the cover of the shade until the hottest part of the day had passed.

And here he was sipping hot coffee. Tim Hortons, to be exact. It had been years since he'd had it, probably not since he'd originally worked the Stump case, back in '93. Lifting the cup to his lips, he took a swig and frowned. He could swear it used to be much better than this. Or maybe he'd been younger then, armed with a less discerning palate. One thing was certain: the donut holes were practically inedible. Dry and fake tasting. Must be that parbaked garbage. It was a sad day when you couldn't trust a coffee and donut establishment to make the donuts in-house. They shipped in frozen, half-baked stuff and reheated it in what essentially amounted to a giant Easy-Bake oven.

He shifted in his seat. Something felt wrong. Something in his gut. Not quite as wrong as his bout with pancreatitis. That hurt like hell. This was more of a general discomfort. Probably the coffee and the two ghastly Timbits he'd choked down before giving up on them, he thought.

But deep down, Loshak wondered if what he was really feeling was guilt for lying to his partner. As if, upon his deceit, a seed of malignancy had been planted in his belly, and now it had taken root and was starting to bloom.

Loshak's eyes fell to the phone resting on the passenger seat of his rental car. He stared at the screen smudged with fingerprints, knowing he should call Darger.

He replayed their last conversation in his head.

"What are you going to Vegas for?" she asked.

"I've got that criminology conference. I told you about it," he said.

"Right. So it's nothing to do with the Stump case?"

Loshak had to concentrate to keep from squirming.

"What would it have to do with Stump?"

"His last known whereabouts happen to be Las Vegas, Nevada."

"Yeah, twenty-some years ago."

"I don't know. Ever since that letter... I guess I keep

waiting for something to happen."

"Well, it's just a boring, old conference, and I won't even be able to tell you about it."

Her eyelids narrowed until she looked like some black-eyed shark. All aggression.

"Why's that?" she said.

He smiled.

"Because. What happens in Vegas…"

The intensity drained from her face.

"Oh. I hate that slogan."

"So do I," Loshak continued. "It's a good place for a criminology conference, though. We're talking about a sex trade industry that rakes in over a billion dollars a year in the city alone. All manner of missing person cases. Human trafficking. The works."

"The perfect place for Stump to hide in plain sight."

He ran his fingers through his hair, resisting the urge to pull some of it out by the roots in frustration. Darger really was like a shark with this Stump case. She could smell the blood from miles away. Why couldn't she just let it be?

"I almost wish I'd never given you the Stump file. Maybe then you never would have mentioned him in the *Vanity Fair* interview, he wouldn't have, uh, reached out to you, and we wouldn't be having this argument right now."

Darger was already shaking her head.

"Feel guilty if you want. Pursuing guys like Stump is my job now. My life. No matter what you or anyone says or does."

He dropped his hand from his hair.

"Suit yourself. You want to keep running around in circles, chasing shadows? Be my guest," he said and got up from his chair. "Toodle-oo, partner. I'll call you from the road."

Many blatant lies, of course. There was no criminology conference. He was here to follow up on leads that may or may not be Stump.

But there was nothing to be done about it. He couldn't have Darger near it until he could be sure.

No, that wasn't true. He didn't want Darger near it at all. Not after what happened in Ohio. And then Atlanta. His partner attracted trouble like a magnet.

Or maybe it was the other way around - rather than trouble coming to her, it was Darger that was drawn to it, like a moth to a candle.

In either case, it wasn't safe. Not with Stump already on her scent like he was. Sending her that letter. The arrogant bastard.

Now, with the artificial chill of the car's AC blasting him in the face, he let his gaze roam over the city, then past it to the mountains off to the west. So much had changed since he'd last been here. So many of the iconic Vegas hotels and casinos were rebranded, rebuilt, or just plain gone. The Desert Inn had been scrapped. The Aladdin was now Planet Hollywood. The one he missed most — the only one that had made him feel any nostalgia at all — was the horse and rider that used to sit atop the sign for the Hacienda.

He didn't know why he should care about something like that. Loshak wasn't one to get sentimental about material things. But he'd always thought of that sign as if it were the official emblem of Las Vegas. Punting the neon horse and rider was like demolishing the Empire State building.

But he was losing focus. He needed to push those thoughts aside and think back to 1993. Back when this had all started.

Stump had killed six women in Colorado, leaving all of them in burned out cars along twisting mountain roads. He disappeared for six months and then turned up with another killing spree in Nevada. The crimes had escalated. Sped up. Verging on berserk, on full-out rampage mode.

It had *spree killing ending* written all over it. Loshak still remembered thinking about that accelerated aggression, discussing it with the other agents and police. There'd been a fatalistic feeling among those working the case. A heaviness in the air all about them. Not only were they powerless to stop the murders, but they felt increasingly threatened themselves, more than a little intimidated. Like all of it would culminate in some showdown, some bloodbath, some careening violent encounter, and they somehow didn't like their odds.

Vegas was a town that was all about the odds, wasn't it?

Crazy and naive as it seemed now, Loshak recalled spending night after night in his motel room, awake in the dark. Peering out the window at the dirt field across the street and wondering if he'd survive this trip.

Lifting the Tim Hortons cup from the holder, he

tried to wash that memory away with a big gulp of now tepid coffee. But the taste of it stayed, lingering on his tongue and throat.

He'd never felt that kind of fear before the Stump case, and he hadn't felt it since. Until now.

CHAPTER 3

November 1993

Claire fights at the zip tie for a second even though she knows it's pointless.

The plastic bites at her flesh. Grooves itself deeper until it looks like a piece of string pinching at a boneless pork loin.

No use. Her wrists may as well be welded together.

But she's doing it. The one thing she mustn't do. She's panicking.

She can't do that. Can't.

He doesn't know she's up. That's the only advantage she has for the moment, and she needs to hold onto it.

She resists every instinct to thrash and claw and scream. Tucks them down as deep as they'll go. And she lies back down. Head nestling in the crook between Tammy's arm and torso.

Steadies her breathing. Narrows her eyes to slits. Watches him through thatched eyelashes.

The back of his head is right there. Dark hair shorn close. Tight and clean.

Everything about him seems clean, in fact.

She can see the shoulders of his sweater. Hunter green. A relaxed fit. Loose at the neck. Almost bohemian. Like something Johnny Depp would wear, she thinks.

The Last Victim

Apart from the pair of Chuck Taylors tipped over on the floor, the sedan is spotless. Impeccable.

Tammy's drooling seems an affront to the atmosphere. A violation.

The thickness of his neck suggests strength and athleticism. He's not all bulked up like some steroid-infested bodybuilder, but he's substantial. A man.

They drive for what feels like a long while. She lets her eyes drift to the rocky terrain and speed limit signs along the roadside, but mostly she stays locked onto him.

Afraid to look away, maybe.

Watching. Waiting.

The whole time she expects that head to swivel around on the meaty neck. Some smirking face locking eyes with her. Revealing that he's watching her. Was always watching her.

But it doesn't. He barely moves at all. Posture rigid. Shoulders stiff.

One of his hands retreats from the wheel. Descending out of view.

A moment later, the click of the blinker taps at the silence.

And they drift out of their lane, and she lifts a little out of her seat. Floating. Floating. Made weightless by the car's movement.

The sedan veers into a Shell station parking lot. Sidles up next to pump number three. Stops.

A lightness flutters at the walls of her chest like the wings of a giant moth.

Blood beats in her eyelids. Hard enough that pink

splotches pulse in her field of vision.

She dares a longer glance away from the back of his skull, gazes out the window, eyes scanning the empty lot and tracing a pole up to the white metal canopy hanging above them.

Empty in all directions. She can't even see a clerk manning the counter inside.

Still, this might be something, right? An opening. A chance. She's not certain.

The car's engine cuts out, and she closes her eyes. Hears the jingle of keys. A soft tinkling in the silence.

And then she feels him turn to look upon her. She doesn't know how she knows at first — does she hear him? Smell him? — but his breathing confirms her instinct.

Air whistles out of his nostrils. Heavy exhales right on top of her. Almost annoyed sounding.

And she smells it then. Alcohol. Bourbon, she thinks.

He must be pretty drunk based on the strength of the odor on his breath, even if there are no outward signs of intoxication in his demeanor or driving ability.

She doesn't move, mind blank though somehow hyper-conscious of the slack flesh of her cheeks as though she might break into some nervous facial twitch if this standoff goes on too long.

The seat squeaks a little when he turns, and then the door opens and slams.

And she can feel his absence. Can feel that his dark presence no longer resides in the car with her.

A bit of the night air swirls over her. A breeze

manufactured by the door's swing. It's cooler and fresher. Almost taunting her.

There's a click and some scraping noises, and then she hears the sound of the gasoline gurgling into the tank. A wet sound babbling under her.

He must be right there. Standing just on the other side of the glass.

Maybe his fingers drum at the nozzle of the gas pump the same way they did at the steering wheel. Maybe he cups the other hand at the glass to cut the glare enough to look on her. On both of them.

Maybe.

When she really tries to picture him, she can only see him standing with his back to her even now. The dark peach fuzz on the back of his head. The loose shoulders of that green sweater.

Faceless, still. A blank slate.

There's a thump, and the liquid sound cuts out as the flow of gasoline ends. He bursts out a few more squeezes, a jerky back and forth of sloshing and thudding, perhaps trying to even things up to a whole dollar.

And then it's quiet.

If he pays at the pump, he'll be back in the car within seconds, though most of the gas stations around here don't have that option yet. The Marathon next to campus does, but… She's not sure about this one.

Wait. Wait. Just play dead a moment longer.

At last she stirs a little, shaking some as she betrays that urge to hold still.

He's halfway across the lot, headed inside. Good.

It's now or never.

Fingers from both hands wrap around the meatiest part of Tammy's arm, and the subsequent jerks make her friend bob up and down, face smearing the back of the seat.

She pauses. Waits.

Tammy doesn't move, so she shakes her again. Harder.

Her whisper hisses between her teeth.

"Tammy. Wake up."

Her lips pop on the plosive at the end of "up," and the rest comes out shrill and harsh.

OK. OK. Think.

She leans over Tammy to grapple at the door handle, fingers scrabbling like spider legs until they find their grip.

She can shove Tammy out onto the pavement, she thinks, and hopefully get someone's notice, even if the lot remains empty.

Would he attack them? Maybe. But she thinks he'd be more likely to speed off while he has the chance.

She hesitates for the briefest of moments as the possible risk runs through her mind, the cold metal stinging the palm of her hand. But there's no debate.

If they get out of the car, they might have a chance. If they stay, they die.

She yanks. Yanks again.

Nothing.

And then she realizes.

Child safety locks. The rear doors can't be opened from the inside.

Fuck.

A new wave of panic rolls over her. Disbelief mixed with a cramping nausea in the middle of her torso.

There's no way to get Tammy out of the car. Not in time.

She leans back. Eyelids blinking rapid fire. Chest hitching and lurching to take in stuttering breaths. She thinks she might be crying, but she doesn't know for sure.

Tammy remains motionless. Crumpled in slumber. Shoulders hunched like a sleeping baby's.

Claire whirls to look out the window. Gazing past the lot. Scanning the yellow lit place beyond the glass.

The dark figure stands in front of the cash register. Again, she can see the shape of his jaw, the square chin. He looks so normal. A face in the crowd. Why is he doing this? Why would anyone do this?

The clerk appears on the other side of the counter, and that snaps her back to reality.

She scrambles for the front seat, her bound limbs not climbing over the barrier so much as wriggling and then rolling her into the passenger seat — a headfirst somersault that lands her on her back.

She flounders there until she can swing her legs around to the driver's seat, and then she flips onto her belly.

In one motion, she hooks her fingers in the door handle, opens it, and her front half spills out onto the asphalt.

CHAPTER 4

September 1991

Claire had always been the quiet type. People often mistook her for being shy, but that wasn't it. She just didn't see a point to speaking unless she had something important to say. She preferred observation and analysis to blurting out an on-the-spot opinion. Besides that, being in the spotlight made her feel awkward.

In short, she was the exact opposite of Tammy, who was a constant chatterbox. Tammy could gab away at anyone who would listen about whatever topic happened to strike her, her arms and hands fluttering all the while. A grand sweeping gesture here. A flap of the wrist there. And a sprinkle of spirit fingers on top.

Some might have thought their friendship odd or unlikely. Even Claire did, sometimes. Other times she wondered if their paradoxical personalities were what made them such a good pair. Tammy would joke that they were like peanut butter and jelly. "Good in our own right, but when you put us together, the magic happens."

They met during their high school's production of *Little Shop of Horrors*. Tammy's bombastic temperament made her a natural stage actress, and she'd been cast as Crystal, one of the three Doo-Wop Girls. Claire was part of the costume department, and her crew chief had assigned her with finding, making, and altering all of the Doo-Wop costumes.

For most of the seemingly endless weeks of rehearsals, Tammy talked and Claire listened, rarely uttering more than a few syllables.

"This morning when I was leaving for school, the woman across the street was on her roof with the leaf-blower."

"Can you turn to the side?" Claire asked, her mouth full of pins.

Tammy swiveled to her left.

"There were no leaves on her roof. There was *nothing* on her roof," Tammy was saying.

One of the other Doo-Wops piped up. "Maybe she'd already blown all the leaves off."

"Nicole, you weren't there. She was leaf-blowing nothing!"

Tammy gazed at her reflection in the mirror and tightened her ponytail.

"My neighbors are all crazy. I think there's something in the water. That's why I won't drink from the tap."

It was a few weeks later — as Claire adjusted a pair of pants Tammy wore in the second act — that they first bonded. She was pinning the crotch seam with Tammy in the midst of one of her sagas.

"So we started picking these little crabapples off the tree, and we noticed that something was sort of raining down on us from the branches over our heads. It took a few seconds before we realized what it was."

Here she paused for suspense.

"Well what was it?" someone asked.

"Spiders. Hundreds, probably thousands, of tiny spiders. Everywhere."

Almost everyone listening recoiled in horror.

Tammy continued, "All three of us just lost it at that point, screaming our heads off, swatting at our arms and faces and hair. My mom came bursting out into the yard, thinking we were being dragged away by coyotes or something."

She flung her arms out to the sides, jostling Claire and coming dangerously close to impaling herself on one of the sharp dressmaker's pins in Claire's hand.

"Hold still for a minute," Claire said. "Or I'm going to stab you in the vagina."

Tammy froze, wide-eyed, staring down at Claire kneeling beside her. Claire didn't know what to make of the reaction at first. Had she offended her with the word *vagina*? Or maybe Tammy had misunderstood, thought Claire meant it as some kind of threat when all she'd been trying to say was that if Tammy kept carrying on, she was liable to get a pin poked in her netherbits. Accidentally, of course.

Tammy was still gawking at her, and Claire thought to herself, *That must be it. She thinks I'm a total wacko now. Great.*

And then Tammy threw back her head and laughed. A big guffaw, straight from her belly.

"What the hell? You haven't uttered word one in — what's it been? — six weeks of rehearsals? And then out pops, 'Don't move, or I'll stab you in the vagina!'"

Relieved, Claire laughed, too. Tammy actually

punched it up a bit, but Claire didn't mind.

Tammy placed her hand on Claire's head.

"You're hilarious!"

Every person that entered the costume room that day got an instant replay from Tammy, and for once, Claire felt like she was really part of the group instead of an outsider watching from a distance.

CHAPTER 5

November 1993

She sucks in lungfuls of that chilly night air, feels the cold touch her insides, suddenly aware that she's been holding her breath for some time.

And her hands reach out, reach out, reach out and touch the rough surface of the blacktop. One hand manages to land flat — the other held sideways by the restraint — and the cool of the ground is immediately absorbed by the meat of each palm.

She balances there and listens a moment, not sure what she expects to hear. Maybe the chime as the glass door swings open somewhere behind her. Regardless, there is no sound but the distant traffic, and even that is sparse. The whoosh of a single car speeding by.

Part of her mind screams for her to hurry now, sure somehow that this will all go wrong.

She lifts her head and the lights catch in the tears in her eyes, smearing everything in refractions, strange geometric patterns.

Her hands crawl forward on the asphalt, carrying her weight, and her legs drag over the seats behind, knees pistoning the best they can to try to help the cause.

The muscles in her legs feel tired. Dead. For the first time it occurs to her that he might have drugged them. Date rape drugs. Roofies. GHB. Something like that. Yes, he must have drugged them, but it's a passing thought as she hurries along.

And she is out of the car. Onto the ground.

The night air envelops her, its chill swirling around her, touching the sweat-soaked places. The cold saturates her to the bone.

She rocks up onto her knees and closes the door behind her. Stumbles into a crawl toward Tammy's door.

Half of her expects it to be locked somehow — like this is some horror movie — but it comes free right away.

She almost can't believe it. This is actually working.

Tammy remains unconscious, even after one more quick shake.

Again she is struck by how much her friend looks like a sleeping infant, all curled up in a position somehow increasingly fetal.

She goes to loop her hands under Tammy's armpits, but she can't. The zip tie won't allow it.

Instead she grabs a wrist.

If she hurries, she can drag Tammy out of the car, and once they're both onto the ground, she can scream bloody fucking murder. There's no one around to actually help — no one but the clerk, at least — so the screaming is more a bluff than anything. Her hope is that he will panic and bolt.

But that also means she can't do it until Tammy is out. Otherwise the panicking and bolting takes her friend away as well.

Claire adjusts her grip, leans back, tries to use her

weight to dislodge Tammy, but it's not working. With her hands stuck together, she can't get the leverage she needs.

She feels like she has tiny Tyrannosaurus arms or something. Little useless chicken wings.

And she sees him now. A shadow in the distance. Pushing the door open. Stepping away from the building.

She yanks again, but it's no good. Tammy's bulk doesn't even shift. The limp arm just flops around.

And some part of her brain seems to click on. Some hyper-aware part meant to record memories in a crisis like this. Some part that knows she's doomed.

Again the tears smear her vision. What feels like sheets of water flushing her eyes and rolling down her cheeks.

She needs to move Tammy, but she can't.

She can't.

She can't.

She can't.

And she has no choice. No options. She won't leave Tammy here.

She climbs over her friend to reclaim her spot in the backseat, closing the door behind her.

CHAPTER 6

October 1991

It was during a Friday rehearsal for *Little Shop* that Tammy cornered Claire backstage during a costume change.

"What are you doing after this?" she asked.

Without waiting for a response, Tammy continued. "Because a bunch of us are going to Big Boy, and you should come."

"Oh," Claire said, somewhat baffled.

Tammy was so loud and vivacious. The kind of person that it seemed like exciting things must always be happening to. She was one of those girls that had friends in every faction of their school, equally at home among the achievers on the yearbook committee, the stoners that snuck joints in the bathrooms, the band geeks, the Homecoming Court.

For this reason, Claire's first thought was, *Me? Why? Is she confusing me with someone else?*

It wouldn't have been the first time. Claire was such a wallflower that some people took no notice of her at all. The previous year, for example, Brad Nichols had turned to her in their 4th period English Lit class and said, "So you're the new girl, right?"

"No," she'd answered.

She and Brad had gone to the same school and been in the same grade for five years now, and her bafflement prevented her from pointing that fact out immediately.

His face scrunched up, like maybe he thought she was lying to him for some reason.

There was probably a new girl in school that looked a little like her, she thought. That was all.

"Your name is Claire, isn't it?"

She nodded, more befuddled than ever.

"And you didn't just move here?"

Now all she could do was shake her head.

Brad shrugged.

"OK, then."

Like maybe he still didn't believe her.

The year that had passed since that incident brought her no more clarity on the subject. There was no new girl at school that she found. And definitely no new girls named Claire.

Tammy was watching her expectantly. That was when Claire remembered the vagina incident, and the interaction suddenly made some amount of sense.

Instead of saying *Yes* or *No* or asking for more details like she supposed a normal person might, Claire said, "I don't have a car."

Tammy ignored the awkwardness of the response, waving it away with a smile.

"You can ride with me."

"OK," Claire said.

And then she floated through the rest of the rehearsal in an almost dream-like state, wondering at how Tammy Podolak had ever noticed her in the first place.

The Last Victim

☾

When they arrived at Big Boy, Claire eyed the statue clad in the checkerboard overalls and thought of the few times she'd been here with her family. They didn't eat out very often. They were too cheap. Or rather, her stepdad was.

On the rare occasion that they did eat out, Keith ordered for everyone, having predetermined what he was willing to spend on the extravagance. For himself, that usually meant a burger platter. Her mother could have the same or the soup and salad bar. Claire always got stuck with the hot dog meal off the kids menu. And she didn't even like hot dogs.

Claire didn't understand what the point of eating out was if they ate the same thing every time. The same thing they could have eaten at home. She longed for just the tiniest sense of novelty.

Every time they were seated and the waitress asked what they'd like to drink, the first thing that popped into Claire's head was, "A Shirley Temple."

Her aunt had ordered one for her once, when they visited her in San Diego. Claire thought she'd died and gone to heaven when the drink arrived in all its bubbly pink glory, with the miniature plastic sword speared through a twist of orange and two maraschino cherries. This fancy-looking drink was for her?

She so wanted to savor it that she almost would have preferred just looking at it. Because if she drank it, then it would be gone. She met herself halfway and sipped at it slowly, a giant grin plastered on her face all the while.

But the rules were different at home. Keith would never allow it. She always asked for water.

On one such night out, after the waitress left to fetch their drinks, Claire asked her mother if she could look at one of the menus.

"You don't need to be lookin' at the menu," Keith snapped.

Claire glanced at her mother. As usual, she wore an expression that was a mix of shame and resignation. Claire didn't know why she expected her to intervene. She never did.

"I thought maybe I could pick something else this time."

He leaned back against the red vinyl of the booth, a bitter sneer on his lips.

"Aren't you just Miss Princess Mollycoddle?"

Keith was not very bright. Claire was only ten, but she'd figured that out early on. He had a handful of these little witticisms that he trotted out when the situation fit. She wondered where he learned a word like *mollycoddle*. It was so bizarrely old-fashioned, and she'd never seen him reading a book.

He turned to her mother.

"This is your doing. No discipline. No respect for her elders. No appreciation for the fact that I slave forty hours a week to keep a roof over our heads and food in our bellies."

Her mom's eyes never strayed from where her hands were folded in her lap. She said nothing.

Satisfied, Keith returned to the real source of his

irritation: Claire.

"You'll have the hot dog meal, and if you've got any sense at all, you'll be happy you're gettin' fed. Money don't grow on trees."

"But all of the kids meals are the same price," Claire blurted.

This was before she'd learned to think long and hard before she spoke at all.

Her stepfather's face turned red. Nothing made him angry faster than being contradicted with sound logic.

Claire winced, bracing herself for his blustering. He'd never struck her, though she could tell he had often wanted to. It was like there was an invisible line everyone knew about and skirted around. Her mother would put up with all of his negative comments, his verbal abuse, his need to control the minutiae of the household, but physical abuse would have been one step too far, and they all knew it.

Keith's meaty hands balled into fists, and he leaned across the veneered table top.

"If I'd been so ungrateful when I was a kid, I would have gone without."

He extended one of his sausage fingers and jabbed the table.

"And then, when we got home, you better believe I'd get a whoopin'."

He shook his head, as if not being allowed to *whoop* Claire was some kind of travesty.

"That's how you teach respect. A hard hand. But no one will do it these days. Just let 'em get spoilt instead."

This last part was directed at her mother again.

Now, seated with Tammy and the other kids from the drama club, Claire was poised to once again order water. But without Keith's suffocating glare, she suddenly realized she could order anything. Whatever she wanted.

And so, when the waitress pointed her pen at Claire, she barely had to think.

"A Shirley Temple."

She heard giggling. Were they laughing at her?

Glancing to her right, she caught two girls from the set design crew smirking at one another. Of course they were laughing at her. How lame was it to be ordering a kiddie drink at her age? Why had she done that? It was a stupid move. Childish.

Claire glanced at Tammy — the only person at the table she could really call a friend — but she was deep in conversation with Debbie.

It was a mistake. Not just ordering the drink but being here at all. She didn't know these people, and they didn't know her. She was an outsider here just like everywhere else. She shouldn't have come.

The next several minutes were filled with tense anticipation. What would happen when the waitress returned with her big pink beverage? Would they laugh more? She wished the waitress would never come back. Would forget about them, and then they'd have to start over with a new waitress, and she could order something normal like a Sprite. Clear fluid. Nothing garish to laugh at there. Nothing anyone would notice at all.

The sound of ice cubes clinking in glasses

announced the waitress' presence. As she rounded a corner, Claire's eyes went immediately to the cherry bobbing atop her stupid drink like a buoy. She stared at the menu in front of her, not having the nerve to meet anyone's eyes.

The group chattered away as the drinks were distributed. The pink thing was set before Claire, and she held her breath.

No one laughed.

It had gone unnoticed.

Thank God.

Claire allowed herself to breathe again.

And then a single voice rose above the rest.

"What is that?" The tone was almost accusatory.

It was Tammy. Claire risked a glance up at her. She was staring at Claire's drink, eyes flashing with amusement.

Oh no.

"It's a…" Claire swallowed, "Shirley Temple."

Tammy threw her head back and laughed.

"Oh my god! I thought so, but I haven't had one of those since I was like nine years old!"

Claire watched the bubbles break on the surface of the liquid and wished she could dive in and drown herself in the pink elixir.

Tammy turned to the waitress, who was waiting for her food order.

"I'll have the chili fries," she said, then crooked a finger at Claire's glass. "And one of those."

Their waitress was an older lady with a perm so tight it looked like a clown wig. She pulled the pen tucked behind her ear and scribbled the new order on her pad.

"Sure thing, honey."

Tammy beamed when the waitress returned with her matching drink.

"A Shirley freaking Temple! Who the hell thinks of ordering a Shirley Temple? You know what you are, Claire? An iconoclast. I can respect that."

Tammy sipped at her drink and then held out her glass. Claire lifted hers, and they tinked them together.

"To new friends," Tammy said.

Claire smiled then, and she didn't think the grin left her lips until Tammy dropped her off at the end of the evening.

CHAPTER 7

Present day

By the time Loshak reached his motel, the sun had set. What he was really here for would have to wait until morning.

He nosed the car into a parking spot near the front office and stared at the building a moment, somehow reluctant to get out.

This was the same place he'd stayed back in 1993. Unlike what he'd seen on his drive through the Strip, this place looked exactly as he'd remembered it. He wondered if he'd get the same room, the same cell to spend his sleepless nights in. Probably not.

He didn't want to stay here. He wanted to do his business and get back to Virginia. But there was nothing to be done about it. There hadn't been an earlier flight.

There was something else, too. Something mingling with the guilt still wriggling around in his gut. It was dread, he knew. Dread that what drew him out here was Stump, even if the hard evidence was flimsy at the moment. Part of Loshak knew he'd be here for quite a while, drawn back into a nightmare from twenty years ago. Trapped in this desert wasteland of sun and sand and sin.

Still he did not move to get out of the car. He picked up the Hortons cup, found it empty, and dropped it back into the holder. The donut holes stared up at him through the gaping mouth of their cardboard container, beckoning him. And for a moment, he considered it. He'd power through them, shove all four down the hatch at once, forcing the horror of fake sweetness and stale pastry on himself just to be rid of them. But no. That would be bad for the ol' pancreas, right? Right. And if he was going to risk his health for a fast food baked good, it wouldn't be for this dog food. No sir. He'd opt to kill himself with lemon pound cake from Starbucks or something a little classier, thank you very much.

A shrill electronic jingle startled Loshak from his confectionery daydream. The phone's screen glowed in the dimly lit interior of the car, showing the name of the caller in bold white text: Darger.

Shit. Should he answer it? He didn't know. Maybe.

His thumb hovered over the screen.

He counted to three and then jabbed the red IGNORE button.

A fresh wave of guilt washed over him. Christ. He didn't know why he felt so guilty about it. It was for her own good. Because it was more than just fearing for her safety. More than keeping her from becoming bait for Stump.

He worried it would get in her head. Worm its way into her brain the way it had his. Take up residence. The Stump case was like one of those parasitic wasps. Just stinging you wasn't good enough. It laid its eggs in you so the larvae could hatch and eat their way out. That's how it had always felt to him, anyway.

The Last Victim

His eyes wandered over to the yellow and red box of donuts riding shotgun. Any remaining urge to choke them down had left him now. He gathered up the box, climbed out of the car, and dumped it in the trash bin on his way inside the motel lobby.

CHAPTER 8

October 1991

The friendship between Tammy and Claire flourished over the next several weeks and throughout the remainder of rehearsals. But Claire worried that when the play was over, they'd go back to being acquaintances that sometimes said *Hi* as they passed one another in the hallway.

The weekend after the play was complete, Tammy called to invite Claire to drive into Vegas for a trip to the mall.

"Who's the ogre?" Tammy asked when Claire picked up the receiver.

"What?"

"The knuckle-dragging neanderthal that answered the phone with a series of grunts."

"Oh," Claire made a dismissive sigh. "My stepdad."

"Does he always sound like that? Like a pissed off cave troll?"

Claire laughed, then said, "Pretty much."

Tammy picked her up that afternoon, and for most of the ride, they listened and sang along to one of the local oldies stations.

During a commercial break, Claire turned the volume knob down.

"What is it that you need?" Claire asked.

Tammy's response was one of befuddlement.

Fourteen creases formed on her forehead. They knew the precise number because she'd spent an afternoon counting the wrinkles in the dressing room mirror while Claire marked the hem length for Tammy's dress.

"You mean existentially?"

"No." Claire chuckled. "From the mall. What are you shopping for?"

Tammy's expression changed to one of theatrical comprehension. Tammy faces were all like that. One-hundred percent, pushed to the max.

"Nothing really."

"Oh," Claire said, like that answer was satisfactory.

But it wasn't. Why were they going to the mall, if not to shop? She'd seen TV shows where kids talked about going to the mall as if it were a popular hangout spot, but she didn't think people actually did that in real life… did they?

She was still pondering this mystery when she realized Tammy had been staring at her for the last several seconds.

"Claire, can I ask you something? And I don't want you to freak out or feel like I'm prying. I just want you to know that you can tell me the truth."

Creeping fingers of discomfort wormed over Claire's skin. What was this about? It sounded like it could only be something bad.

"OK," she said, her curiosity only slightly more intense than her dread.

"Are you an alien?"

Claire grinned, saw that Tammy was only half-joking, and then giggled.

"No. I'm not an alien."

While some people might have been offended at the implication, Claire knew Tammy well enough now to know that meeting an actual, honest-to-goodness being from outer space would have been her dream come true. It was the furthest thing from an insult coming from her.

As it was right now, Tammy had on a pair of earrings with little green alien faces on them.

"That's just what an alien would say, you know."

"Because if I *was* an alien, I obviously wouldn't be able to tell you."

Tammy smirked at her, like she knew Claire was only playing along and trying to pull her leg, but she was also half-hoping it was true.

Of the several malls in Vegas, Tammy chose one away from the strip.

"Too many tourists down there," she said.

She parked the Mustang in the Macy's lot, and they headed inside.

Claire was used to shopping with Keith, who would bark at her if she so much as looked at something for too long. In contrast, walking through the store with Tammy was endlessly amusing. Her friend touched everything, purring like a cat as she pet a faux fur coat or holding up a sequined top in front of herself and then shimmying back and forth to watch the shifting sparkles. Sometimes she'd pause and engage in a one-sided conversation with one of the mannequins.

"Oh Barbara, your ass looks fantastic in that

pantsuit!"

After testing half the bottles at the perfume counter, Tammy coughed and waved a hand in front of her nose.

"Fragrance overload!" She nabbed Claire by the sleeve and pulled her toward the promenade. "Come on. Let's go to Orange Julius."

"What's that?"

Tammy halted, not minding the glare she received from a woman pushing a stroller that had to move around them.

"You've never had an Orange Julius?" She was incredulous.

Claire shook her head.

"That's it. You're totally an alien. Undeniable evidence," Tammy pronounced.

She started walking again. "We have to rectify this immediately. How else can you report back to your planet on the many wonders of planet Earth if you haven't had an Orange frickin' Julius?"

At the food court, Claire took her place next to Tammy in front of the kiosk with a giant orange lit up with neon lights. A surly girl with severely drawn-on eyebrows took their order and prepared the mystery concoction in a pair of industrial grade blenders.

Claire sipped at the frothy orange beverage while Tammy watched, waiting intently to gauge her reaction.

"Good, right?"

Claire nodded.

"Tastes like a melted Creamsicle."

"Exactly!"

At another booth, they procured soft pretzels, and then they sat, sipping and chewing and people-watching.

Claire felt strangely grown-up for once. Something about being in this place, surrounded by people, far away from her mom and stepdad. No one knew her here. Well, except for Tammy. But she could be anyone to the rest of them.

And being with Tammy was like being on a ride at an amusement park. People seemed to notice them. Boys watched them. Smiled at them. Claire was pretty sure they were mostly looking at Tammy, but still. It was like Tammy had some kind of magic magnetism that drew the eye.

Claire studied her friend and realized that part of the magnet was Tammy's smile. She beamed at everyone. Grinned at perfect strangers as if they might be old friends.

She spent a long time trying to find words to describe that particular sensation she got while hanging out with Tammy. Eventually, she decided that it felt like anything was possible.

CHAPTER 9

November 1993

Again she watches through woven eyelashes. Concentrates to snuff out the impulses to cry, to whimper, to shake and heave and tremble and jerk.

The dark figure slides into the driver's seat, and he hunches over the wheel as he cranks the key in the ignition.

The engine hiccups once before resuming its one-note song.

She doesn't think. Not really. Her mind functions on some primal level now.

She observes, waits, watches. All of her consciousness existing moment to moment. Like a frightened animal.

If he'd seen her movement as he walked to the car, he shows no sign of it.

The dome light was on when he returned — evidence of her opening the doors, of course — but he doesn't seem fazed by this. Doesn't seem to notice at all.

His hand moves to the gear shift. Grips it.

He glances back at them then. His expression blank. Almost like he's not really looking. Going through the motions while his mind resides elsewhere.

It happens so quickly this time that she doesn't even consider closing her eyes that last little bit before he's facing the other way again. He doesn't acknowledge it, in any case. Maybe with her eyelids narrowed, they looked closed. She's not certain.

He puts the car in drive, and they're moving again. Gliding out of the lot, away from the building, away from the lights.

The car bobs to and fro as he guides it onto the road, but the movement steadies, and it feels familiar. Oddly calming. Like a ship cruising the seas, riding higher as it accelerates, moving out into dark water.

The deep.

They follow the glowing trail that the headlights blaze for them.

And nothing else moves out there. The night is still. Quiet.

Her elbow prods at Tammy's ribs again. She doesn't expect a response, and she doesn't get any.

But it's OK. The ride helps her gather her wits. Helps her get ahold of herself.

They will get another chance. She knows it. Wherever he takes them, they will get another chance. Because this car will stop eventually. And that will be it.

She will fight. She will scratch. She will claw.

She will get away or die trying.

They both will.

He clears his throat in the front seat.

"Hey," he says.

His voice is deep. Textured. Almost raspy, but somehow smooth in spite of it.

She closes her eyes. Feels her heart beat faster in her

chest.

"You. I saw you."

Again she gets that feeling in her face — almost like an itch — all of those muscles in her jaw and cheeks want to twist and flutter and spasm.

"I know you're awake. I take it your friend is still out, eh?"

She squeezes her eyelids tighter. Tries to hold back the tears that want to gush out just now, spill down her cheeks.

"Not in the mood to talk, are you? I can understand that, I suppose. Though I'm afraid I'll have to insist. Just for a moment."

She feels the car slow and pull over onto the shoulder, gravel pinging against the undercarriage.

The drone of the engine changes, goes slightly higher as he shifts into park, and then it holds. She thinks it'll falter to silence any second, but it doesn't. He leaves it running.

After a long moment, he speaks again.

"I knew you wouldn't run. You never would, would you? You wouldn't leave her."

The wet spreads down her cheeks now, collects at the corners of her mouth, warm and salty, and she's vaguely aware of the tremor jolting her torso. A stirring in her middle that cannot be calmed.

"Your friend there'll go first. You understand? You will watch. And once you see everything — all of it, all of the ugliness, all that happens and doesn't happen — you won't want to run anyhow. Not at all. Not at all. You won't want to run or walk or think or breathe.

You will ask me to finish it. Beg and plead. You will be ready to go, and I will free you of your pain. You understand that?"

He's quiet again, and after a pause, she hears his fingers drumming once more on the steering wheel. The beat he keeps is slow. Totally out of time with the racing patter of her heart. There's something hypnotic about it.

Her eyelids flutter open, and the green lights from the dash look harsh through the lens of her tears.

He still doesn't face her straight on. His head cranks back about halfway, and shadows drape the side facing her and she can't discern the eye in the dark.

"Why?" she says, her voice small and tight and strange in her ears.

"What's that?" he says.

The beat on the steering wheel stops, and his eyes turn to meet hers in the rearview mirror. At first they look like deep black pits, but he adjusts the mirror and they look normal. Totally normal.

"Why are you doing this?"

His gaze breaks from hers, and his eyes shift off to the right. He blinks a few times. Slow blinks that remind her of an intelligent dog.

"Because… Because nothing here makes sense until…Because nothing here is real until it's written in flesh and blood. That's why."

He reaches into the backseat, and she freezes when she sees it.

The blade in his hand.

It's like it just appears there. Drawing closer. The

metal glinting in that pale green light from the dash.

The knife's edge kisses the flesh between her lip and jaw, soggy with tears. So sharp she doesn't feel the slash until his hand moves away again.

And the skin pulls apart. The wound opens. And the first wave of blood seeps down her chin. Hot and thick.

CHAPTER 10

March 1992

Spring came, and all anyone in the Senior class talked about was college.

"Do you know what you're doing for school yet?" Tammy asked her one day.

Claire shrugged.

"Probably I'll go to UNLV. Where else?"

Keith had protested her going to college at all. Said they couldn't afford it. But Claire's mom insisted on it. It was one of the only times she'd ever seen her mother stand up to him. When she found out he'd been taking part of Claire's paycheck from her summer job as a lifeguard, she made him pay back every cent. That was Claire's college fund, she said.

"But for what?" Tammy asked.

"For my major? I've been thinking about accounting."

Tammy's jaw dropped.

"Accounting! Why?"

Claire shrugged again.

"I'm pretty good with numbers. I figure everyone needs an accountant."

Tammy's head shook back and forth so fast her hair was a blur around her face.

"Claire, no! No, no, no! I won't let you do that."

"Do what?"

"Throw away your talent to do something snooze-worthy like accounting!" She crossed her arms. "I mean, if you really liked it, fine. But you don't, do you?"

"Not really."

"Then I ask again. *Why*?"

Claire didn't have an answer.

"Why wouldn't you go to school for fashion design? You're good at it. And you love it. And oh! Lightbulb moment!"

Tammy was always having lightbulb moments.

"Once we have our degrees, we'll both move to New York City where we'll get famous and rich and be the stars of Broadway!"

Claire raised her eyebrows in doubt.

"Not right away, of course. I mean, we'll have to start out at the bottom, naturally. We'll get a shitty little roach-infested apartment together, because it's expensive as hell to live in the city, you know. And we'll slog through the smaller theater companies. But eventually... eventually, super stardom will fall right in our laps. I know it will. We'll both have a whole shelf of Tony awards in our fabulous Manhattan penthouses — by then we'll have upgraded from the dingy little apartment. People will come from all over the world to intern under you and learn all of your costuming secrets. Meanwhile, I'll be featured in the tabloids and gossip mags every other week. Wild speculation about my very public break-ups with Patrick Swayze and Christian Slater. Rumors of a whimsical drug problem."

Claire raised an eyebrow.

"Whimsical?"

"Well, it's always a *serious* drug problem, you know? I want mine to be fun."

Tammy stared out the window at the passing scenery: an endless repeat of withered grass, scrubby little trees, and the foothills in the distance.

"Honestly? It doesn't even have to be as fantastic as all that. I'll be happy just to get out of this damn town."

She turned to Claire.

"Sometimes at night, I start worrying. You know my mantra is *Shoot for the stars*, but what if I never get out of here? What if I'm just stuck, and this is it? This is all I was ever meant for?"

Claire smiled at her friend.

"I don't believe that. I kind of think you had it right with the super stardom falling in our laps thing."

Tammy clapped her hands together and grinned.

"So it's a deal then? We'll be roommates, and you won't major in something boring that you'll end up hating yourself for?"

Claire laughed.

"Of course it's a deal. Who am I to stand in the way of destiny?"

CHAPTER 11

Fall 1993

She and Tammy were practically joined at the hip that
first year at UNLV. They went to orientation the same
weekend and signed up to live together in the dorms.
On the weekends, they went to coffee shops to study.
Neither one of them was very used to caffeine, but it
made them feel grown up and important. So they
drank cappuccinos and cafe lattes, nibbled at scones
and croissants, and always ended up jittery and buzzed
by the end.

For Christmas, Tammy bought her a pair of really
fancy sewing scissors with gold plated handles. It was
such a classy gift, and Claire knew it had to be
expensive. It made her own gift seem silly by
comparison. But Tammy still squealed with delight
when she opened it.

"It's perfect! Where on earth did you find it?"
Tammy's eyes narrowed. "Or maybe that's just it. You
didn't get it *here* at all, did you?"

It was a Best Friends necklace, the kind that broke
in two halves so they'd each have one to wear. Instead
of the standard heart, this one was shaped like an
alien's face and glowed in the dark.

Tammy pulled her half over her head and handed
the other piece to Claire.

When summer came, they moved out of the dorms

and into an apartment. Tammy wanted to decorate, though her exact words were, "I've got a Martha Stewart bug up my ass or something." And so they went to the fabric store and picked out material. Claire sewed curtains for the windows and little cushions for the chairs at the built-in breakfast nook, all in shades of red, Tammy's favorite color. Red car, red lipstick, red dress, red heels. That was Tammy.

Tammy even managed to get Claire to loosen up enough to get drunk a few times. The idea of Claire at a bar or keg party probably would have made her stepdad's head explode if he'd found out. Of course, even the slightest chance of Keith's ogre skull bursting almost made telling him about it worth it.

Claire remembered one party — some friend-of-a-friend of Tammy's — when the cops burst in and started handing out citations to anyone under 21. Tammy grabbed Claire and pulled her into a coat closet, along with six or seven other people. They were crammed in like pickles in a jar.

Pressing her mouth to Claire's ear, Tammy whispered, "I am so high right now."

She giggled, and someone shushed her.

"What's happening?" asked a voice from further back in the closet.

Claire was closest to the door, but the only thing she could see was the sliver of light let in by the crack at the bottom of the door.

"I don't know. I can't exactly see through the door."

"Well, can you hear anything?"

Her eyes were finally adjusting to the dark. As

Claire pressed her ear to the wood, she saw that the guy standing next to her was doing the same.

At first all Claire could make out was indistinct mumbling, but eventually some of it became clear.

"Is that everyone from upstairs?" The voice was sharp and authoritative. A police officer, she assumed.

"Yeah. I mean, I guess so," was the response.

"What about the basement?"

Claire kept her voice low as she relayed what she'd heard.

"They're trying to find out if they missed anyone. So we can't make any noise."

"Oh no!" Tammy squeaked.

More shushing from the back of the closet.

"What?" Claire said.

"If they find us, I'm in super duper big trouble."

Tammy was still talking too loudly.

"We'll all be in super duper big trouble if you don't shut up," Claire said.

"Yeah, but you're only drunk! I'm drunk *and* high. That's, uh, twice as much trouble, right?"

"They won't know that."

"Yes they will. They'll smell it on me! Oh god. Can you smell it on me, Claire?"

Before Claire could stop her, Tammy blew a big puff of her breath at Claire's face.

"There! Does my breath smell like weed?"

The hot air from Tammy's mouth was all yeasty and tangy from the beer she'd been drinking. Claire's nose wrinkled.

"It doesn't smell like weed."

"Why'd you say it like that?"

"Like what?"

"I have bad breath, don't I? What's it called? Halitosis."

Tammy snorted and repeated the word, drawing out the O and S sounds.

"Halitooooosisssss."

"Will someone shut her up?"

"You shut up," Claire snapped at whoever was talking.

"What's going on outside?" Came another voice. "Are the cops gone yet or what?"

Claire leaned forward to press her ear to the door again.

Almost instantly, Tammy's voice came from behind her.

"Does anyone have any mints?"

"Oh my god. Shhh!" said the whiny person in the back of the closet.

There was a tap on her shoulder.

"Claire, do you have any mints? Or gum? You always have gum."

Claire sighed and stepped away from the door.

"In my purse."

"Where's your purse?"

"On my shoulder, but I can't really get to it the way we're mashed together in here."

"I'll get it," Tammy volunteered.

Claire felt Tammy's hand inch its way down from the strap on her arm to where the bag rested at her hip.

With Tammy properly distracted, Claire pressed

her face to the door once again. The guy next to her was also listening. The voices were too muffled to make anything out, but it sounded like the police were still there.

"Can you hear what they're saying?" the guy asked.

"No," Claire said.

"Success," Tammy exclaimed in the dark. "Altoids!"

The tin rattled as Tammy opened it, and then there was a metallic clank and the sound of a few dozen mints scattering on the ground.

"Oops!"

The murmuring voices outside suddenly halted. Heavy boots stomped over the wood floor, moving closer to the closet, and all Claire could imagine was the door being yanked open by one of the policemen and finding them hiding inside. Would they be angry that they hadn't come out? Was that considered resisting arrest? Claire didn't know.

In the dim light, she could see the face of the boy standing next to her. His eyes had gone wide in the dark, probably a mirror of what her face was doing right now.

"I'll—"

Claire didn't know how she found the space to do it, but she spun around and clapped a hand over Tammy's mouth. The group in the closet seemed to instinctively hold their breath. No one moved.

After five seconds that seemed more like five hours, the footsteps outside receded. She released her hold on Tammy and relaxed a little.

"I spilled them!"

"I know, Tammy. It's OK."

"I should pick them up. It would be rude to leave a mess like that."

"Just leave them for now. There isn't room."

"But they'll get squashed under our feet! A curiously strong powder."

Before Claire could stop her, Tammy had forced herself into a squatting position, jostling everyone around her to make room.

Claire's door buddy suddenly grunted and buckled at the waist. She thought he might be about to vomit, and she reached for his elbow to steady him. And also to keep him pointed away from her in case he was about to blow.

"Are you OK?"

It was a moment before he could answer.

Finally, in a choked whisper he said, "Yeah, but... she elbowed me in the balls."

The cops never did find them. A few minutes later, Claire heard the front door slam shut and their heavy tread thunking down the front steps.

The group filed out of the closet and ended up hanging out with the few stragglers that hadn't been sent home. The guy Tammy cracked in the nuts introduced himself to Claire. His name was Kyle. A few weeks later, he became Claire's first serious boyfriend. And now, some months later still, he also held the distinction of being her first ex-boyfriend.

That was part of the reason she was out on a Thursday night in the first place instead of waiting for the weekend. She wasn't a heavy partier, usually. Not the way Tammy was. But she'd been pretty upset about the break up, and Tammy had been working on her for a good two weeks.

"Forget him. You need to get back on the horse."

"I prefer men," Claire said.

"Ha. Ha. You know what I mean. Let's go out. It's Dollar PBR night at The Mystic."

Claire didn't even like the taste of beer, but she'd drink it because it was cheap. And she liked the way it made her feel mellow, more so than hard liquor. When the alcohol hit after taking a few shots or downing a Long Island Iced Tea, it was like getting hit with a sledgehammer of drunkenness. Heavy and fast. But beer felt like a slow relaxing flutter that made its way from her chest up to her head. And there was a certain appeal to getting drunk enough to stop wallowing in her post-breakup self pity.

On the drive to the bar, Tammy had the radio on full blast and tuned to 94.9, aka Buzz 95, The Alternative Rock Powerhouse. Tammy was next to her, bopping her head to the beat, singing along to Nirvana and They Might Be Giants. Claire was lost in thought, face angled to look out the window at the multicolored lights and neon signs streaking by in the night. Tammy suddenly turned on her.

"Dude!"

Tammy's mouth was pulled back in a sneer of mock outrage.

"What?"

"Where the hell are you? I need you belting the Layne parts, or it doesn't feel right!"

It was a moment before Claire realized what Tammy was talking about. And then she heard it. The song on the radio was *Man in the Box* by Alice in Chains. It was one of their favorites and always elicited a good twist of the volume knob when it came on. They had come to an unspoken arrangement in which Claire sang the Layne Staley parts while Tammy backed her up with Jerry Cantrell's vocals. They were already mid-way through the first chorus.

"Sorry. I wasn't paying attention."

"No duh."

"I was thinking about — "

"I know what you were thinking about. Or rather *who* you were thinking about. Now quit it. Tonight is about forgetting him. We're going to have fun tonight, damn it. The whole future is wide open, right? Anything is possible."

Claire must have looked unconvinced.

"Right?" Tammy asked pointedly.

"Right," Claire said, because the look Tammy was giving her said she didn't have a choice.

Tammy gestured emphatically at the car speaker. Claire took a deep breath, shaking her head, and then started to sing along.

With a grin and nod, Tammy joined her.

By the end of the song, Claire was grinning too, and she thought maybe Tammy was right. Maybe it was time to move on. Time to forget Kyle.

Anything was possible.

CHAPTER 12

November 1993

Blood weeps from the wound. A diagonal trickle draining into her mouth.

She presses the sleeve of her sweatshirt against the opened place. Watches the heather gray cuff go damp and red.

The car barrels forward again. Rocketing through the emptiness.

The man in the driver's seat has fallen quiet now that they are moving once more.

There is a tension to him she didn't recognize before. A hostility she can read in the arc of his shoulders, the furrow of his brow, the puckered lines around his mouth. Maybe it wasn't there at first. Maybe it didn't really exist until he spoke to her, tried to communicate whatever that was.

She senses a frustration. Some nebulous notion that he was trying to say something to her and couldn't find the words. That maybe he tried to say it with his blade after that, etch it into the skin along her mouth, and he came away disappointed with that attempt as well.

He didn't kill her, though he could have. A similar slash to her throat would have done it, within minutes more than likely.

And that was his mistake, she thinks.

Because she is still here, and whatever else might

happen, she is more determined than ever to fight until the end.

She puts her weight on the balls of her feet, pumps her calves a couple of times. She thinks the feeling is coming back into her legs, thinks that the effects of whatever drug he slipped into their drinks must be waning some, at least for her.

Good. Good.

An empty sprawl lines the sides of the road now. They turned off the main road a while back. There are no gas stations or fast food places out here. No neon lights or street lamps. Just the hard red rock and thick shadows as far as she can see.

Her elbow keeps working at Tammy's middle, though it's mostly out of habit at this point. She does it without thought, the idea of Tammy waking no longer a real possibility in her mind.

"The cabin is just up here," he says, his voice deeper now, almost sleepy sounding.

She can hear the smile in his words as he goes on.

"I know I don't have to say it, but you be good now. Both of you. I don't want any trouble making our way inside. I mean that."

The car slows, takes a right turn.

A steep, overgrown driveway slashes tire tracks into the dust, and the car shimmies a little as they trample some dead weeds and bounce their way through potholes and eroded places in the dirt trail.

The engine seems to grunt a little as they crest a rocky incline, and she sees it.

The dark building just ahead. Small and

ramshackle. Sun bleached wood siding. Yellowed newspaper over the windows the color of rotten teeth. A cluster of juniper trees lean against the structure, their silhouettes looking like stooped figures.

She should be terrified, she thinks. Crying. Groveling. Squirming.

But she feels no fear. Only an overwhelming desire to act. To fight. To fucking survive. No matter what.

He doesn't know her as well as he thinks he does.

And for just a second as the car begins to slow, she has a strange moment of clarity. She sees all of those memories added up, sees the whole of her friendship with Tammy, the whole of both of their lives.

And she sees how incredibly small they are, how fragile. Vulnerable beings in a mindless, violent, raping world.

Just as the car rolls up next to the cabin in slow motion, she pounces.

She dives into the front seat, rolling as before, but this time she's prepared for it.

She lands on her back and kicks. Feels her feet connect with that head she's stared at for so long. Feels it throttled on that meaty neck. Hears the side of the skull thud against the driver's side window.

And her fingers find the handle without hesitation this time. The door pops open, and she falls out onto her ass, scratchy tumbleweed clawing at the flesh of her arms, dry and dead.

She scrambles to her feet, a huge cloud of vapor congealing all around her as her breath hits the night's chill. His dark shape writhes at the edge of her vision, exiting the car.

She flees into the hills, swallowed up by the pitch black nothing, and the dark figure follows.

CHAPTER 13

Present day

Loshak woke to the sound of a kid throwing some kind of tantrum just outside his motel room door. His hand fumbled around on the bedside table for a few seconds, searching for his watch. Finding it, he brought it close to his face to read the dial. Not quite half-past eight.

He replaced the watch and let his eyes roam around the room. It wasn't exactly the Ritz: dingy carpet, faded wallpaper, a cigarette burn or two on the arms of the sofa.

He didn't mind it so much, really. They didn't make them like this anymore. The whole place had a blast-from-the-past vibe going on. Even the customer service seemed more of the 80s and 90s than now. When he'd been waiting for the clerk to get him his room key, the desk phone rang. Instead of answering with the name of the motel and asking, "How can I help you?" the man simply said, "Yeah?"

Loshak had gotten a chuckle out of that. Everything was so homogeneous now — so clean and corporate — that a little bit of indifference was almost endearing.

He rolled onto his back and blinked up at the ceiling. All in all, he'd slept better than he thought he would. Maybe that was one of the perks of getting old. Your body wore down on some higher level, gave way to slumber whether you were happy or mad or stressed.

Maybe that's what death will be like, he thought. Your thoughts may still lurch and sway in your head, but your body slows until you slip away to the deepest slumber of all.

That thought made him think of Shelly. His eyes flicked over to the framed photograph he always brought with him when he traveled.

She was eighteen in the photo. Young and bright and just figuring out the person she would become.

The kind of girl Leonard Stump liked best, he thought. Like a raccoon ransacking a peach tree, he took one bite and left the rest to rot.

((

Steam coiled out of the black plastic lid of the Tim Hortons cup. He almost didn't know why he'd gone there again. But his palate seemed to crave that particular brew once more, demanded it, even if it wasn't what it used to be. At least he knew not to trifle with the donuts this time around.

Once more, his eyes flicked over to where his phone rested in the passenger seat. He could tell by the red blinking light that he had a voicemail message. From Darger, no doubt.

He hadn't listened to it yet. Couldn't. Not until he'd done what he came here to do. And then he would call his partner and tell her everything.

The brakes of Loshak's rental car let out a low groan as the car came to rest in front of the small house. The yard was more dirt than grass, with a row of yucca around the foundation that kept it from looking completely barren. But for the most part, the whole place had a sad, grubby look to it.

He knocked, trying to keep it light and neighborly, knowing how the person on the other side of the door surely hated unannounced visitors.

There was a window to the right of where he stood, the blinds drawn against both the sun and prying eyes. Two of the slats parted ever-so-slightly, and Loshak knew he was being watched. Just as quickly they snapped shut again.

He counted, imagining the person inside with one hand on the door knob, trying to decide whether or not to open it. He understood the impulse of not wanting to. If their positions were reversed, Loshak thought he might go right back to his business and pretend he'd never noticed someone at the door at all.

It was a full seven seconds before he heard the rattle of a chain and the thunk of a deadbolt. The door opened wide, squealing a bit at the hinges. Through the screen that still stood between them, Loshak saw her. The girl who got away.

Even if not for the distinctive scar on her chin, he'd know her anywhere, no matter how many years had gone by. It was her eyes, he thought. Not just the warm brown color of her irises, but the look in them. In the brief moment when their eyes first met, Loshak caught a glimpse of the fear. A flash of utter dread, of suffering, of a lifetime of looking over her shoulder.

Because she remained Stump's victim even still. She

lived it on and on and on.

And then the fear retracted, the curtains drawn over the fear, and she smiled a little.

"It's you."

It was a practiced smile. A smile that wanted to convince you that things were OK, that she was OK. But Loshak knew better.

He knew that beyond the smile and under the fear, there was something that made it so the world would never be OK for Claire Garcia. A terrible knowing of the things men are capable of.

"It's been a long time," he said.

"Yeah. The years go by fast, but the days are long. Or that's how it feels to me anyway," she answered.

Loshak felt a little stab in his chest. He'd always liked this one. She didn't talk much, especially not back when it first happened, but when she did, she had a way with words.

Neither one of them spoke for a few seconds. They just stood and studied one another through the haze of the screen door.

"Is it him?" she asked finally.

So she knew then. It didn't surprise him. Not really. If anyone aside from him would have that sense, it would be her.

"I think it is."

"And you think I can help?"

Straight to the heart of it, as always.

"No one else knows it like you," Loshak said.

Something that was half-wince, half-smile tugged at the corner of her mouth for half a breath, pulling her scar so that a series of tiny puckers appeared along the edges. Just as quickly, it vanished.

"Do you remember what you promised me? When he first escaped?"

Loshak swallowed, feeling like the resulting sound was exaggerated to emphasize his discomfort.

He nodded. "I remember."

He'd promised he would find Leonard Stump. That he wouldn't rest until the man that had taken her and killed her best friend was locked behind a steel door and ten inches of reinforced concrete.

He'd been young then. Naive enough to assume the good guys always won. Arrogant enough to think it would be easy to track Stump down. Thoughtless enough to believe he could make a promise like that and keep it.

She bobbed her head once, perhaps glad that he hadn't offered some kind of excuse for failing her.

"Well... I guess you better come in, then."

She pushed the screen door open a few inches. Loshak caught the handle, pulled it wide enough to step through, and disappeared into the house.

CHAPTER 14

Claire found her way to the highway that night and managed to flag down a minivan, an awkward task with her hands bound at the wrist.

An already frazzled night got very, very blurry after that.

These days the only images she really remembers are the glare of the headlights and the face of the driver that stopped to help her — a man who looked remarkably like Santa Claus. White beard. Glasses perched at the very tip of his nose.

He drove to a gas station two exits down the road, and she was so out of sorts that he had to call the police for her from the pay phone.

Within two hours, Loshak and the other investigators had interviewed her, and it was the information she provided that led to Stump's arrest some 14 hours later.

Police set up roadblocks forming a radius around the area where Claire had escaped, and an officer at one of the checkpoints spotted a pair of pink converse All-Stars in the backseat of a Mercury Sable. The owner of the vehicle was taken into custody.

Stump gave only a PO Box as his local address, but police turned up the cabin some hours later. His prints were everywhere along with what looked like several weeks worth of trash shoved in a small shed behind the main building. A few small items among the garbage could be tied to other local victims.

At last, the world had a face and a name to attach to these awful crimes.

Leonard Stump.

The national media swarmed anything and everything involving the case. They plastered his face everywhere.

Claire managed to avoid most of the spotlight by refusing all interview requests, despite the tenacity of the media. She had to change her phone number three times. Loshak kept in touch with her during the buildup to the trial.

But there never was any trial.

Six weeks after the arrest, Stump escaped while at the Carson City courthouse for a preliminary hearing. It was believed that he climbed out of a bathroom window, using a stolen winter coat to avoid notice on the street as he slipped away.

Sometimes the simplest escapes are best. It reminded Loshak of Ted Bundy jumping out of a second story window and stealing a car.

The eastern edge of the Humboltd-Toiyabe National Forest lies less than two miles from that courthouse. Along with most of the other investigators, Loshak figured Stump fled into the park and used the many cabins and camping areas to evade the numerous search parties that pursued him throughout the winter of '93. When Spring came with no fresh signs, they gave up. And while some of the investigators floated the idea that Stump might have perished somewhere in the forest, Loshak always knew better.

Tammy Podolak was never found — living or dead — though most assumed her to be Stump's last victim. Until now.

THANK YOU

Thanks so much for reading *The Last Victim*! Want more Darger books? Leave a review on Amazon, and let us know.

A NOTE FROM THE AUTHORS

Unfortunately, Amazon won't automatically flag you down when there's a new book in the *Violet Darger* series. Don't miss out!

Take one of the following actions to make sure you're always among the first to know what Darger and Loshak are up to:

1) Sign up for the Vargus/McBain email list and never miss a new release. Just visit: **http://ltvargus.com/mailing-list**

2) Follow one of us on Amazon. Just click the **FOLLOW** button under my picture on my author page, and Amazon will send you an email every time we have a new release.

3) Join our Facebook Fan group and chat with us about books and movies and all that good stuff. We'll let you know when we have something new. Join here: **http://facebook.com/groups/mcbainvargus**

ABOUT THE AUTHORS

Tim McBain writes because life is short, and he wants to make something awesome before he dies. Additionally, he likes to move it, move it.

You can connect with Tim via email at tim@timmcbain.com.

L.T. Vargus grew up in Hell, Michigan, which is a lot smaller, quieter, and less fiery than one might imagine. When not click-clacking away at the keyboard, she can be found sewing, fantasizing about food, and rotting her brain in front of the TV.

If you want to wax poetic about pizza or cats, you can contact L.T. (the L is for Lex) at ltvargus9@gmail.com or on Twitter @ltvargus.

LTVargus.com

Made in the USA
Las Vegas, NV
22 November 2024

12407656R00051